③ Croaked

The electrifying serial continues . . .

In *The Slobberers*, when Rory's mum and Dawn's dad went missing on their honeymoon, Rory and Dawn set off after them. But at every turn they were chased by bone-sucking slobberers.

In *Battering Rams* Rory went on the scariest, smelliest ride of his life while Dawn got rounded up by some very strange and nasty sheep. Dawn's dad was still missing, but they couldn't search for him now. Not when their own lives were in peril.

What is going on?

Is a strange sickness creeping over the land? Or is the step-family spreading a disease of its own?

Read on. *Croaked* will grab you.

Wicked!

③ **Croaked**

Paul Jennings and Morris Gleitzman

PUFFIN BOOKS

PUFFIN BOOKS

Published by the Penguin Group
Penguin Books Ltd, 27 Wrights Lane, London W8 5TZ, England
Penguin Putnam Inc., 375 Hudson Street, New York, New York 10014, USA
Penguin Books Australia Ltd, Ringwood, Victoria, Australia
Penguin Books Canada Ltd, 10 Alcorn Avenue, Toronto, Ontario, Canada M4V 3B2
Penguin Books (NZ) Ltd, 182–190 Wairau Road, Auckland 10, New Zealand

Penguin Books Ltd, Registered Offices: Harmondsworth, Middlesex, England

First published in Australia by Penguin Books Australia 1997
Published in Great Britain in Puffin Books 1998
5 7 9 10 8 6 4

Set in Cheltenham

Made and printed in England by Clays Ltd, St Ives plc

British Library Cataloguing in Publication Data
A CIP catalogue record for this book is available from the British Library

ISBN 0–140–38992–X

ONE

My new house had never seemed less like home.

Gramps and I stared out of the kitchen window. The plague of frogs was still there.

The frog general ate his little soldiers one at a time. He chewed and chomped and sucked and swallowed. And with each mouthful he grew bigger.

The line of frogs shuffled forward like troops waiting for the firing squad. They jumped into his gaping gob without complaint. Without protest. They were sacrificing themselves. But for what?

The frog general was as big as a dog and still growing. The smaller frogs had failed in their attempt to get into the house. So now they were joining forces.

1

Making one big frog. That could . . . could . . .

Break down the door.

This was crazy. Crazy, crazy, crazy. The frogs could have attacked me on the road. But they had gone right past. Jumped over my head. So who were they after?

It could only be one person. Gramps.

'We have to stop that frog,' I said in a trembling voice.

'Rory,' said Gramps, 'did you know I was a Rat?'

Oh no. He was rambling again. Out of his mind. Now he thought he was a rat.

'The Rats of Tobruk,' he said proudly. 'In the war. We held Rommel off for months. I was in the Tank Corps.'

I tried not to get upset by Gramps' nonsense. The frog general had grown to the size of a sheep. And the line of frogs was leaping faster and faster into his gaping mouth. They reminded me of bullets being loaded into the breech of a gun.

'I wouldn't mind a tank right now,' I said to Gramps. 'We could blow the frog general away.'

Gramps began to chuckle. 'I've got one,' he said. 'I've got a tank. Out the back.'

Oh, it made me sad. It really did. Poor old Gramps.

I had been seeing a few things myself lately. But that was because the slobberers had licked my cut hand.

The infection had spread right up my arm and onto my chest. Sometimes it made my head spin and sent me crazy. I saw things that weren't there.

But Gramps had some other problem. He was off the planet all the time. I never knew what he was going to do next. Not that it made any difference to how I felt. I really liked him. He was a great guy. He was Dawn's gramps, not mine. But he and I were growing close. In the heat of battle. Comrades in arms.

My thoughts turned to Dawn. She was really gutsy. Big, strong and bold. And dead? Oh, I hoped not. I would have given anything to see her walk through that door. I started to feel really mean for calling her big bad Dawn. After all, the step-family was just as bad for her as it was for me.

'This'll fix him,' said Gramps.

I looked up and saw Gramps holding a large sack of salt.

'Frogs and snails and things don't like salt.' He started to laugh and chuckle like a mad man. 'We'll lob it into his gob.'

I peered out through the green-splattered windows. The general was still cannibalising the company of frogs. His webbed feet were as big as hubcaps. He certainly wouldn't have any trouble smashing through a window.

'Not a bad idea,' I said slowly. 'But how will we get the salt out there without them attacking us?' The thought of the general's slimy mouth made me shiver. We had to do something though. Sitting waiting for the general to invite himself to dinner wasn't my idea of fun.

Slam. The back door banged.

'Gramps,' I screamed. 'Gramps. Don't go out there.'

I was too late.

I rushed to the back door and threw it open. I couldn't see any frogs because they were lining up in the front yard. And I couldn't see Gramps. Where was he?

'Come on, Rory,' said a muffled voice. 'Start her up. We'll let him have it.'

Where *was* Gramps? What was he up to?

The voice was coming from the vegetable garden. The wheelbarrow. A large metal dustbin was sitting in the wheelbarrow. Suddenly the lid of the bin popped open and Gramps' head poked out. He was wearing a pair of goggles and pointing towards the front yard. Oh, weird, weird, weird. Gramps thought the wheel-barrow was a tank. He was back in the Second World War. Attacking the enemy.

'Oh, what the hell,' I yelled to myself. 'We've got to do something.' I raced into the garden and pushed

Gramps' head back inside the bin. 'Stay there,' I said. 'Until I tell you.'

'Charge,' came Gramps' excited voice from inside the bin.

I grabbed the handles and started to push the bin around to the front yard. Gramps was heavy but there was a slight downhill slope. And the cement path made it fairly easy. Faster and faster. There. There they were. The tiny frogs were still leaping to their doom. The general frog was still gorging himself. I gasped. He was as big as a full-grown cow.

The general took no notice of me. Neither did the line of frogs. They must have been too intent on what they were doing. Or hadn't they seen me?

I had no time to think as I headed down the path towards the general. The wheelbarrow started to wobble from side to side. I couldn't keep it upright. 'Tank traps,' came Gramps' muffled voice. 'Keep going.'

I was nearly there. I stared into the frog general's huge, gaping mouth. I looked into his cruel eyes. They were as big as soccer balls. They swivelled and he fixed me with a wet glare. He started to roll his tongue back into his mouth. I knew without a doubt what he was going to do. He was going to slurp me up and slide me down his throat.

'Now,' I screamed. 'Fire.'

Gramps' head popped out of the bin and the general forgot all about me. His rolled tongue was already coiled like a spring. Gramps' shaking hands held the sack of salt in the air but it was too heavy for him. He began to sink down into the bin. *Thwack*. The frog general cracked out his tongue like a giant whip just as Gramps' head disappeared into the bin.

The general's tongue plucked the sack from Gramps' hands as if it was no more than a fly sitting on a leaf. In a flash it was gone. Swallowed.

The wheelbarrow tipped over and we both fell sprawling onto the ground. 'Land mine,' he yelled. 'A blasted landmine.'

We stared up at the frog. For a moment the world seemed to stand still. Nothing moved. Then the general began to moan. His pimpled green skin started to stretch. His bloated body bulged and quivered.

Bang. The frog general exploded like a monster balloon that had been pricked by a pin.

Thousands of bits of green muck hurtled into the air. Then they began to fall. Green and brown goo dripped down over the lawn and the house. Shreds of dead frog covered my hair and windcheater. The gum trees seemed to bear rotting green fruit.

'Yahoo,' yelled Gramps. 'We got him. The general's

croaked it.' He did an excited little rain dance on the lawn.

There were a few thousand frogs left still standing in line. They seemed paralysed by the loss of their leader. For a few seconds they just stood there. Like a queue at McDonald's that's just heard the hamburgers have run out.

Gramps danced away in front of them. But he was celebrating too soon.

I stared at the blasted bits of the frog general which covered the landscape. They began to writhe and squirm. They were growing little legs and eyes. The pieces of the general were turning into more frogs. Thousands of them.

'Quick,' I screamed. 'Back to the house.'

But I was too late. The frogs were already heading there themselves. Leaping and bounding like a swarm of lumpy locusts, they spread across the lawn and poured into the house.

They ignored Gramps. They ignored me.

So what were they after?

Gramps and I waded through the door. The frogs were swarming into Mum and Jack's room. They were into the clothes cupboard. They were all over Mum's jeans and wedding dress.

Then it hit me.

RORY

The frogs were not after me. They were not after Gramps.

They were after Eileen. My mum.

TWO

I **was huddled in a** rickety roadside fruit stall, about to die. Killer sheep with razor-sharp steel wool were thundering towards me on a bone-crushing tractor. To make things worse, I was hugging a step-mother I didn't even like.

I should have been praying.

I should have been screaming for Dad.

Instead I was having shameful thoughts.

I remembered the earlier sheep attacks. With the fork. And the rake. And the wrecker's ball. All aimed at my step-mother.

It's Eileen they're after, I told myself, not me. I could run for it. I could sprint down the road and they wouldn't even see me go. They'd be too busy stabbing Eileen and ploughing her into the ground.

I peeped through a crack to see if I had enough time to get out. Yes. The tractor was several seconds away. If I flung open the

9

door and ran, I could make it.

Now.

Do it now.

I didn't move.

Instead I stared at Mum's shoe, lying where I'd dropped it on the dusty road in front of the advancing tractor.

I couldn't leave Eileen. She might be a pain. She might have stolen Dad from me. But she was Rory's mum.

Then an amazing thing happened.

The sheep saw the shoe. Their eyes widened. Their stiff steel wool, gleaming in the morning sun, seemed to bristle.

Just before the tractor ran over the shoe, one of the sheep pushed at the steering wheel with its front legs and the tractor swerved.

It thundered past the fruit stall. The walls shook. Eileen swore. We were showered with dust and old price tickets.

I kicked open the door and peered out, just in time to see the tractor veer across the road and hit a large rock.

All four sheep flew through the air. Three of them crashed down into the undergrowth. They scrambled to their feet, leaves and twigs impaled on their wool, and glared at me. Chest thumping, I waited for them to charge. But they didn't. They glared a bit more, then turned and ran off down the road.

I looked around anxiously for the fourth sheep. At first I couldn't see it. Then I heard grunting and looked up.

The sheep was halfway up a large tree, the steel wool on its back embedded in the trunk, its legs sticking out in surprise. It started to kick and snort. After a while it tore itself free and fell to the ground.

From that height it should have been history. It wasn't. It stood up, gave me an evil look and came towards me.

My insides went rigid with terror.

Then I had an idea. I picked up Mum's shoe and pointed it at the sheep.

The sheep stopped. It took a step backwards. For a few seconds it seemed to be frozen. Then it turned and ran off down the road, a large scab of bark still stuck to its back.

I hugged Mum's shoe, weak with relief.

But I was puzzled. Why had the sheep swerved? Why had they all run off? Was it just that they didn't like dead people's footwear? Or did Mum's shoe have some sort of special power?

My thoughts were interrupted by Eileen staggering out of the fruit stall. She had a price ticket in her hair – 2.99 a kilo. She looked shocked and dazed and her sling was crooked and I felt pretty bad that I'd thought of nicking off and leaving her.

Sometimes you had to take responsibility for people even though it was your dad who'd invited them into your life.

'The sheep have gone,' I said. 'For now.'

Eileen nodded slowly, her eyes darting around. She seemed to be having trouble taking stuff in, even really short sentences.

I went over to the tractor. It had flipped over and was sitting in a puddle of diesel, wheels still spinning. I'd thought perhaps we could ride it back to town, but the engine looked pretty crumpled.

Then I heard a faint sound.

Soft and high-pitched.

Baa.

I tensed and gripped Mum's shoe.

Baa.

I looked around frantically. Was there a fifth sheep with a dodgy voice, about to drop out of a tree?

Then I saw it. Huddled near the tractor. A tiny lamb, about three days old. It had something wrong with its leg and looked like it was in pain.

Normally I'd have picked it up. I'd nursed quite a few

injured lambs in my time. Dad reckoned I had the touch.

But when those sheep on the wrecker's ball had turned to steel, part of me had too.

'Go on,' I said to the lamb. 'Shoo.'

The lamb didn't move. Eileen came over. 'Poor little thing,' she said. The lamb baaed pitifully and looked up at her with big eyes.

Eileen picked it up.

'Be careful,' I said, wondering if I was turning into one of those people who couldn't feel sympathetic even in sad movies.

'You poor love,' said Eileen to the lamb. 'What's wrong?'

I saw instantly what was wrong. As Eileen cradled the lamb, its soft fluffy white wool was turning hard and grey and steely.

'Eileen,' I yelled. 'Let go.'

I swung Mum's shoe and knocked the lamb out of Eileen's arms. It landed on four strong and perfectly healthy legs. The needle-sharp coils of its steel wool glinted.

'You little scumbag,' I hissed. Before I could point Mum's shoe at it, the lamb sniggered and ran off down the road in the same direction as the others.

'Are you okay?' I asked Eileen anxiously.

She was dabbing at her neck. She looked at her fingers. There was blood on them.

'I'm okay,' she said. 'It's just a scratch.' She wiped the blood off.

I waited for my own blood to stop pounding in my ears.

'Come on,' said Eileen, heading off down the road. 'I want to get home and find out what's happened to Jack and Rory.'

I hurried after her. How could she be so calm? I'd already explained to her that Rory was probably dead. And the fear slicing through me was that Dad was too.

Suddenly I felt sick with grief.

I squeezed my neck muscles and decided that Eileen was right. No sense in panicking till we knew for sure.

'Good idea,' I said. 'They're probably fine.' My neck knew I was lying and cramped up. I had a sudden urge for a curried-egg sandwich to make it feel better.

I made myself think about other things.

'Eileen,' I said, catching her up, 'the sheep are after you, so you should carry this.' I pushed the shoe into her hand. 'It was Mum's. She was wearing it when she died.'

Eileen stared at it. 'Yuck,' she said, and dropped it.

Okay, it was dirty and mildewy, but what did she expect from a shoe that had been to the bottom of a river and then in a wrecked bus for five years?

I picked it up and tucked it inside Eileen's sling. 'It'll protect you,' I explained. 'The sheep don't like it.'

'*I* don't like it,' said Eileen, thrusting it back at me.

I saw in her face what she really meant. 'I don't like your mum,' was what she meant. 'I don't like her because she was a drunk or a mental case or both and she crashed a school bus with my son on it.'

I took the shoe back. 'One day,' I said, my eyes pricking with tears, 'when we've sorted out all this weird stuff, I'll find out the truth about my mum's death and then you'll have to apologise.'

We trudged towards town, not speaking.

Two things happened on the way.

After about ten minutes I noticed some piles of brown powder on the road. Five of them. Each pile was about the size of a sheep, except for one which was much smaller.

I bent closer.

It was rust.

I stuggled to make sense of what I was seeing. Could Mum's shoe have done that? Turned the sheep into rust?

The second thing happened close to the house. I'd just noticed that Eileen's neck seemed red and swollen where the lamb had scratched her.

Eileen suddenly turned to me, wide-eyed and scared.

'What's this?' she said, pointing to her sling.

At first I didn't understand what she meant.

'What is it?' she shouted.

'It's a sling,' I said, suddenly scared myself. 'You and Dad had a car crash and you hurt your arm and made a sling out of one of Dad's shirts.'

Eileen stared at the shirt. Then she gave a relieved sigh. 'That's right,' she said. 'I remember.'

Poor thing, I thought. She must have concussion. At least we'll be home soon.

To calm myself down I thought of our place, just over the next rise. At the top of the hill I stopped to gaze down at the familiar cosy house nestled among the trees.

Instead I stared in horror.

The last time I'd seen the house it had been white. Now it was green. Green walls, green roof, green guttering, green windows.

And even at that distance I could see that the green was alive.

THREE

It **was awful.** Disgusting really. To see those frogs swarming over Mum's clothes. The foul green plague filled sleeves and legs and pockets. The frogs filled out flat jackets and jumpers and made them ripple and flow with a dreadful life of their own.

'The mongrels,' yelled Gramps. 'They've got us outnumbered.'

He wasn't wrong there. I started kicking and jumping and squashing the frogs under my shoes. But it was useless. There were just too many. The green tide grew higher as the frogs climbed on each other's backs to get at Mum's outfits.

Gramps tugged at my shoulder. 'Come on,' he said. 'We need to talk.'

We waded out to the kitchen where there were fewer frogs.

'The first question is,' said Gramps, 'are they really there? Or am I getting confused again?'

'You see them,' I said. 'And I see them.

So they must be there.'

'Well, the next question is,' said Gramps. 'What do they want?'

'Mum,' I said. 'They are all over her clothes. It's *her* they want.'

Gramps looked terribly upset. And I was scared. For some reason it was worse now that Mum was in danger and not me. Scared for yourself is one thing. But scared for someone you love. That's different altogether.

By now almost all of the frogs had swarmed into the bedroom. We could see them from the kitchen. They were piled up in one huge seething mass that reached to the ceiling. They reminded me of a heap of tiny green sumo wrestlers struggling for prizes.

I started to tremble and shake all over. Like someone who has malaria. It was all too much. I just couldn't take any more. I needed someone to wake me up. And hold me in their arms. I was only a kid. Mums and dads are supposed to fix things up. To look after you. To make the nasty things go away.

But how could they help me? I had driven them all away. Suddenly I felt all alone in the world. Everything seemed to be my fault.

Dad had gone away and left me years ago. Why didn't he come back? Was it because my leg was twisted and I couldn't walk or run properly any more? Was he disappointed because I'd never play football for Essendon like he wanted me to?

And Dawn's mum. Dead. Drowned in a bus. I couldn't remember what had happened but I probably caused that too. No wonder Jack and Dawn didn't like me.

But that wasn't all. No – I had to go and put some slobberers in the stew and cause Jack and Mum's car to run off the road. They were probably dead as well.

Was there anyone I hadn't hurt? I had run out on Dawn. Left her to be chased off into the night by the slobberers. She was probably nothing but a sucked-out scruffy doormat by now. All because of me.

I was no good to anyone. No one wanted me. And I didn't blame them. Right then I wished I was the one who was dead.

Without warning two arms grabbed me. It was Gramps. He hugged me close to his chest. Tears ran down my cheeks and soaked into the wool of his jumper. I could smell that musty odour that all gramps seem to have. We just stood there hugging each other without speaking.

A hug doesn't need words.

Finally I stopped shaking. I opened my eyes and wiped my damp cheeks. 'Look,' I shouted. 'Look.' I saw something wonderful. Fantastic. Better than winning the Lotto. Better than a Ferrari. Better than anything. I was so happy.

I could see two figures walking down the track towards the house.

So could the frogs. They started to pour out of the bedroom and into the hall.

I was filled with joy and terror. It was Mum. And Dawn. They *weren't* dead.

'We have to keep the frogs in the house,' I shrieked. 'We have to. They'll kill Mum. It's her they want.'

I ran through the frogs to the back door and slammed it. Then I ran back to the window. 'Stay away,' I yelled desperately at the distant figures. 'The frogs are after you.'

The frogs surged towards the windows and doors. Gramps started kicking at them. He slipped and slid around on the greasy floor. His legs were tottery but he stomped and stamped like crazy. 'We need re-inforcements,' he yelled in a horrified voice. 'I can't hold the line. The scumbags are breaking out.'

But he was wrong. We didn't need help. Even through the mist of my terror I could see that something was happening. The frogs were not their old selves. The fight seemed to be going out of them. I noticed that some were already dead, while others waved their legs at the ceiling like huge green beetles turned on their backs. The fittest of them were hopping half-heartedly towards the door.

'I don't believe it,' gasped Gramps. 'They're giving up. Just when they had us beaten.'

I tried to work out what was happening to the frogs. It was almost as if they had lost interest in Mum.

By the time Mum and Dawn reached the garden gate every frog was dead.

I rushed out of the door and threw myself into Mum's arms. 'You're alive,' I screamed. 'You're alive, you're alive, you're alive.'

'Where's Dad?' Dawn shrieked at me. 'Is he with you?'

I wished I could tell her that Jack was alive, but I didn't know where he was. And anyway, I couldn't speak. Mum was kissing the top of my head and pushing my face into her soft body.

Gramps started hugging Dawn. 'He'll turn up,' he said. 'He's missing in action. Probably a prisoner of war.'

'Slobberers don't take prisoners,' said Dawn. 'Neither do killer sheep.'

'Killer sheep? Killer frogs, you mean,' I said.

Mum frowned at me. 'Don't you start on that nonsense too,' she said. Then she turned to Gramps and hugged him. That was really nice to see but I couldn't really enjoy it. It is a terrible feeling when something wonderful happens at exactly the same time as something awful. I was so happy to see Mum. She was thrilled to see me. Dawn was pleased that Gramps was okay. And I was rapt that Dawn had not been slurped up by slobberers. Dawn even looked as if she might be glad that I was still alive.

But none of us could be really happy while Jack was missing.

We all walked slowly towards the house, Mum hanging on to me. And Gramps hugging Dawn. We stared at the goo that dripped from the eaves and gutters. It looked as if a furious green snowstorm had attacked our home. In amongst the slime you could make out an occasional bit of frog – an eye or leg or a bit of rotting curled tongue. But mostly it was just slimy gunk draped over everything.

'What happened?' whispered Dawn.

'Rommel's green panzers,' said Gramps. 'But we licked 'em. Me and Rory and the other Rats of Tobruk.'

'Frogs,' I said. 'They were after Mum.'

'Like the sheep,' said Dawn. 'They were too.'

'Don't you start on that,' said Mum angrily. 'I've heard enough about slobberers and killer sheep and . . . other nonsense for one lifetime.'

At that very moment I saw something that made my

heart fill with fear. As Mum grew angry, a purple bruise started to wash up her neck.

Mum sat down in a slimy green chair.

'Oh, yuck,' said Dawn.

Mum didn't seem too worried about the goo. 'Where's Jack?' she mumbled. 'My head feels funny. I can't remember things.'

I felt a hand in mine. A soft, warm girl's hand that sent a pleasant little shiver up my spine. I looked up at Dawn. It was funny. If you sort of half closed your eyelids and squinted at her from the side, she really was quite pretty.

'Come on,' said Dawn. 'We have to talk, Worm Boy.'

Worm Boy? I pulled my hand away and stomped outside after her.

We went into the garage and Dawn sat on the wood pile and glared at me. 'My dad's missing,' she said. 'I want to know what's going on.'

'Okay,' I yelled. 'Okay, okay. I know it was my fault. But he still might be alive. We have to do something. We're the only ones who know the truth. No one will believe us.'

'What *is* the truth?' she said.

'Slobberers,' I said. 'And frogs and maggots. And a dead goat come back to life. And . . .' Dawn's eyes grew wide as I told her everything that had happened. Well, almost everything. I couldn't tell her that I had seen her mother in the old bus. That couldn't have been real. We all knew she was dead. That bit must just have been my sick mind.

Then Dawn told me about the giant slobberer. And the killer sheep. And everything else she had gone through. Her story was worse than mine. She was pretty brave was Dawn. You had to give her that.

What had happened was awful. But she left the worst till last. 'Your mum can't remember about the sheep,' she said. 'Even though she saw them. And she doesn't believe me about the slobberers. Or you about the frogs. She's sick.' Dawn pointed at my hand. 'And so are you.'

I gave my head a shake and tried to clear my muddled brain. 'We have to stick together on this,' I said. 'Mum's in trouble. Jack must be too. We have to stop fighting each other and start thinking.'

'Yes,' said Dawn slowly. 'We have to piece the bits together. Where did the sickness begin?'

I held up my aching arm. 'The slobberers licked me,' I told her. 'I've got slobberer's disease.'

Dawn looked at me carefully. Did she shuffle back a bit? Was she scared of catching something? Or was that just my imagination?

'Yes,' she said. 'You've got an infection all right. But

what about the sheep? The slobberers licked you. And . . .'

'I could have infected the sheep. I stuck my cut finger up a sheep's nose. Then other sheep might have been infected.'

'And gone off hunting for Eileen.'

'Like the frogs,' I yelled. 'A frog licked my cut hand. Then infected frogs came searching for Mum.'

'The lamb,' shouted Dawn. 'The lamb pricked Eileen. That's how she got infected. The disease goes from person to creature. And creature to person. The slobberers infected you. You infected the sheep.'

Suddenly Dawn grabbed a stick and started scratching in the dust on the garage floor.

'What are – ?'

'Quiet,' she said. 'This is complicated.'

I bit my tongue and watched her as she drew.

'The worms infected you,' she said. 'And you infected sheep and frogs. And now the sheep have infected Eileen. And now she'll infect other animals. Maybe cats or dogs or ...'

I couldn't take it in. I didn't like the sound of it. I didn't want to believe it. 'Why are the infected animals all dying?' I said.

'It's like sperm,' Dawn blurted out.

I blushed. Even in the middle of all that trouble I blushed. Jeez, she had a big mouth.

'What are you talking about?' I said.

Dawn drew again in the dust. Just like a sex-education teacher at the blackboard. 'Thousands of sperm go for an egg,' she said. 'But only one gets through.'

'I know all that stuff,' I said gruffly. I did too. In fact I'd been thinking about it a fair bit lately.

'And,' said Dawn. 'Once the egg is fertilised all the other sperm just die.'

'So?' I said.

'So it's the same with slobberer's disease. Once the person they are after has been infected, the germs have no target and the creatures all die. Their job is done.'

I thought about it. She could be right.

'Then the infected person passes it on to another

creature,' I said slowly. 'And a whole lot more of them catch it. And they go looking for . . .'

'Someone else in *your* family,' said Dawn, sounding a bit relieved.

A shiver ran through me. My family? Who else could that mean?

Dad, that's who. Was I going to kill him too? With my germs?

I held up my bruised arm. 'Do you think I will keep passing it on?' I said. 'Can I still infect animals that will go searching for my relatives?'

'I don't know,' said Dawn slowly.

Suddenly I had an idea. I ran over to Jack's tool shelf and picked up an old plastic box. I ran outside and searched around in the bushes. 'Got you,' I yelled.

'A snail?' said Dawn. 'What do you want that for?'

I put the snail under the tap and watched it as it stuck out its little eye stalks. I rubbed the snail's face into my wound so that it would catch the germs. Then I placed it in the box and put on the lid. We could see what the snail was up to because the lid was made of clear plastic.

We both peered down at the snail. It moved around for a bit and then pulled its eyes back into its shell.

'We'll watch it,' I said. 'If I'm infectious and can

still pass on the disease . . .'

I didn't finish the sentence so Dawn did it for me.

'The snail will start to change,' she said.

FOUR

I **felt a bit better,** knowing Dad couldn't be infected.

But only a bit.

He could still have had his bones sucked out by a slobberer or his skin scraped off by a mean-minded sheep. I was aching with worry. Where was he? Why wasn't he here?

I did what Dad always did when he was worried sick. Kept myself busy.

Rory and I went back to the kitchen and I made everyone their second hot drink in a row and tried to occupy my mind by wondering what exactly the infection was and whether Eileen would turn into a slobberer.

I could see Gramps was worried too. He kept looking at Eileen and Rory, his face crumpled with concern. But he didn't want to alarm them, so he tried to stay cheery.

'Top tea,' he said after a couple of sips. 'Better than the pot I made.'

'Thanks, Gramps,' I said. He was right, mostly because he'd used gravy powder.

'Goes right through you,' he said, 'tea. 'Scuse me.' He shuffled off to the bathroom.

I was in the middle of wondering which I should do first, ring the police or make Eileen and Rory have a lie-down, when a familiar voice filled the kitchen.

'Jeez, am I glad to see you lot.'

I spun round.

Dad was leaning against the door frame, face streaked with dirt, shirt torn, jeans filthy, smiling wearily. He opened his arms wide.

'Dad,' I screamed, and rushed at him. But it wasn't me he wrapped his arms round, it was Eileen. I stood waiting, grinning, heart thumping with joy, desperate for my turn.

'Where have you been?' asked Eileen tearfully.

That's exactly what I would have asked.

'Twisted my leg,' said Dad. 'Tried to take a short cut back to town along the old fire break. I was that rope-able with myself for pranging the car I didn't watch where I was going. Stepped in a wombat hole. I've done more crawling in the last sixteen hours than all the pollies in Canberra put together.'

I grinned even wider. Good old Dad. Now he was here everything would be okay.

Eileen stepped back and anxiously checked Dad over and I slid in for my turn. I put my arms round him and hugged. He ponged of B.O. but I didn't care. My eyes were watering anyway.

'Oh, Dad,' I whispered. 'I thought you were a goner.'

He didn't reply. I looked up at him. He was staring at Eileen, concerned. She did look pretty crook. Her neck was red and blotchy and her face was sort of grey.

There was so much to tell him, I hardly knew where to start.

'Something weird and terrible's happening, Dad,' I began. 'There's an infection and Rory and Eileen have got it and it turns grubs into monsters and sheep into killers.'

I realised he wasn't even listening. He was still staring at Eileen. 'Jeez, love,' he was saying to her. 'We've got to get you to a doctor.'

'I'm okay,' she said. 'It was only a scratch.'

I pulled at Dad's arm. 'Listen to me,' I pleaded. 'We were attacked by giant worms. Huge giant worms. And sheep on a tractor.'

Dad was staring at me now. Not with concern, with irritation. 'Dawn,' he said sharply. 'You can see what Eileen and me have been through. We're having the world's crookest honeymoon and this is no time for games.'

'It's not a game,' I yelled. 'It's real.'

I heard Rory stand up at the kitchen table behind me. He'd been quiet till now. The infection seemed to do that to people. Now he stopped being quiet.

'She's right,' he said angrily. He pointed to the purple bruise on his arm. It was growing even as we watched. 'The slobberers did this,' he said.

Dad stared. 'Jeez,' he said. 'You look worse than your mum. Must be some sort of stress reaction.' He spoke softly to Eileen. 'Has your family ever had a skin complaint like this before?'

My head felt like it was going to explode. What was happening? Why wouldn't Dad believe me?

I turned frantically to Eileen. 'Tell him about the sheep,' I pleaded. 'The tractor. The wrecker's ball.'

Eileen stared at me, puzzled. There was a long pause. 'Tractor?' she said finally. 'Wrecker's ball?'

'The sheep on the wrecker's ball,' I yelled. 'You were there. You saw it. You were infected by a steel lamb. Tell him.'

Eileen looked confused. 'Steel lamb?' she said, staring at the floor. 'I can remember the explosion, and the car skidding ...'

'Dawn,' said Dad with rising anger, 'this is not the time for these games.'

Frustration and panic exploded in my guts.

'Come on,' I screamed at Eileen. 'Get real. It was less than two hours ago.'

'Dawn,' roared Dad. 'You do not speak to Eileen like that.'

'Leave her alone,' Rory yelled at Dad. 'She's just trying to tell you what's going on, you stupid idiot.'

Eileen slammed her coffee mug onto the table.

'Rory,' she said furiously. 'Apologise to Jack this instant.'

Suddenly everybody was shouting at everybody. I yelled at Dad that he was pig-headed. Then I stopped. I realised what was happening. Another type of disease was sweeping through the family. We'd been infected with it the day Dad and Eileen got the hots for each other, but we'd never had as bad a dose as this before.

I saw what the anger was doing to Rory and Eileen. The more worked up they got, the more the purple blotches on their skin quivered and bloated. And it was making their faces change too, just for short spells. A couple of times I could hardly recognise them.

Then Rory yelled at Dad that he was pig-headed, and I wasn't going to put up with that.

'None of this would have happened if you weren't such a grub, Worm Boy,' I yelled. 'Carrying around rotting apples and pockets full of filthy worms.'

Eileen glared at me icily. 'That's good,' she said,

'coming from a kid whose bed is a dumping ground for half-eaten biscuits and mouldy toast crumbs.'

'Fair go,' said Dad. 'The first time you and Rory stayed here I found half a pizza in his bed.'

Eileen's blotch gave an angry twitch. 'Why is it,' she said, 'that when Rory and Miss Perfect here do exactly the same thing, Rory always gets bad-mouthed?'

'Because,' said Dad heatedly, 'pizzas stain and biscuits don't.'

Eileen laughed bitterly, 'Oh yes, you'd know all about that. You who haven't made a bed once in the fifteen months we've been together.'

'Haven't made a bed?' roared Dad indignantly. 'The first time I slept at your place the sheets had so many holes in them I had to go out and buy a new pair.'

Eileen stared at him.

'You never bought new sheets,' she said.

'Two pairs,' he said.

Eileen frowned. 'No, you didn't,' she said.

I stared at Eileen. I'd seen those new sheets with my own eyes.

'I see,' said Dad, furious. 'And I suppose when I hopped into bed and you said I looked like the bloke in the sheet ad, that didn't happen either.'

Eileen frowned again, then glared. 'No,' she said.

'My mistake,' yelled Dad, pulling open the back door.

'You must have thought I was someone else.' He hobbled out, slamming the door behind him.

I followed him out.

He was sitting on a stump staring at the lawn. I put my arm round him.

'Let's go somewhere,' I said. 'Start a new life. Just you and me.' I hadn't planned to say it, but when it came out I realised I meant it.

Dad gave me a squeeze. 'Love,' he said softly. 'I know all those tales about monster worms and crazy infections are your way of telling me you're not happy. I get the message you think Eileen and Rory are a bit of a plague. But I need her. After Mum died I was as empty as this poor blighter.'

He picked something up and brushed ants off it. I realised with a stab it was the dry flat body of the magpie that the slobberers had sucked out.

'There was nobody around to save this poor bloke from the ants,' said Dad. 'I was lucky. I had Eileen to save me.'

I opened my mouth to tell him it wasn't ants that had emptied out the magpie. But before I said a word I knew I wouldn't be able to convince him. Not about the slobberers or leaving Eileen.

A cry came from inside the house.

'Help.'

It was Gramps. I rushed in. Gramps was sitting on the dunny, the door open, yelling hysterically. 'It attacked me,' he shouted. 'A giant worm.'

Eileen and Rory got to him first. By the time I'd sprinted down the hall, Gramps' cries had turned to quiet sobs.

'A giant worm,' he sniffled.

'It's okay, Wilf,' said Eileen gently. 'It's just the draught excluder.' She held up the cloth tube filled with sand we used to stop draughts whistling under the dunny door.

'Don't worry, Gramps,' said Rory. 'It's scared me a few times too.'

While they comforted Gramps, I noticed an amazing thing. The blotches on their skins were shrinking.

'I'm just a dopey old man,' sobbed Gramps.

'No you're not,' said Dad, hobbling along the hall. 'Anyway, a bloke doesn't have to be old to be dopey.' He turned to Eileen. 'Sorry I blew my stack,' he said softly.

Eileen looked at him and frowned. 'Did you? I don't remember.'

Dad put his arms round her. As I watched them hug and kiss, I realised that for all their good qualities, me and Rory couldn't depend on them to get to the bottom of the weird and scary stuff that was happening.

And if our own parents wouldn't believe us, the police and the army certainly wouldn't.

It was up to us kids.

FIVE

For a second or two I had thought that Mum and Jack were going to bust up. But no such luck. After the big row everyone settled down and went back to abnormal. Mum and Jack were as thick as thieves again. All lovey-dovey.

I showed Mum the remains of my mouse and she just said, 'Poor thing. Must have died of stress, listening to you two fighting.'

Dawn didn't fare any better when she showed them her sucked-out fish. 'That's a shame, love,' said Jack. 'But the only slobberers around here are you two at

tea time.' Mum and Jack both laughed like crazy. Parents can be maddening sometimes.

Dawn and I went outside and dug two little graves. I put my mouse skin in the bottom of one and Dawn slipped her flat fish into the other.

'Say a few words,' said Dawn.

I bowed my head over the graves.

'Nibbler,' I said. 'You were happy until you got into a step-family.'

'So were you, Finger,' said Dawn.

'You didn't really want a step-fish but you put up with it,' I said.

'Same for you, Finger,' said Dawn. 'A step-mouse is just like a step-brother. Painful.'

I cleared my throat. 'But then you both got sucked out by slobberers. We know you had a terrible end to your short lives. But now you can rest in peas.'

'Peace, idiot,' said Dawn. 'Rest in peace.'

'I know that,' I said in an embarrassed voice.

I picked a white onion-weed flower and threw it into Nibbler's grave. Dawn threw a buttercup on top of Finger and we filled in the two small holes. Then we went into my bedroom where we could talk.

The snail box was on the bed next to my apple-man. Dawn stared at the snail. It was safely tucked up inside its shell and nothing was happening.

'It doesn't look infected,' said Dawn. 'I don't think you're contagious. But I reckon your mum probably is. She's going to infect an animal, and then it's going to go looking for another one of your relatives. Who will it be?'

I didn't want to think about that. 'What will carry the germs?' I said. 'Mosquitoes? Or ants? Or wombats? Or kangaroos? Or elephants? It could be anything.'

'What *I* want to know, Worm Boy,' said Dawn, 'is where this germ or whatever it is came from in the first place.'

I felt sick in the stomach. I couldn't think about that either. I didn't want to face the thought. When you don't want something to be true you can pretend that it's not. But in the end it gets to you. Like a slobberer in an apple. In the end it will come for you.

Dawn was never one to beat around the bush. She took a deep breath. 'Your dad,' she said. 'Your dad sent the slobberers in your apple-man present.'

'He didn't,' I screamed. 'The slobberers were only normal grubs. They probably got infected in the mail. Or after I got the apple-man. Dad wouldn't send slobberers after me. I'm his son. He wouldn't. He could be the next victim. We have to find him.'

'Okay,' said Dawn. 'Keep your shirt on. You could be right. But it's up to us. We are the only ones who know what's real.'

'But some things *aren't* real,' I said.

'Like what?' said Dawn.

'Like the bus getting new again. Like the goat coming to life. Like the flies and the maggots. Like me seeing your mum.'

It slipped out. It just slipped out.

'What?' shrieked Dawn. She sprang up into the air like a demented cat. 'You saw my mum? Don't be ridiculous. How dare you. You must be out of your mind.'

'That's what *I* thought,' I said. 'It's the disease. It makes you see things when you get upset. Hallucinations. Like a nightmare. That's what happened on the bus.'

Dawn calmed down a bit.

'My mum's dead,' she said sadly. 'I saw her body in the funeral parlour. Her hair was all wrong. And they put a horrible shade of lipstick on her lips. But it was her all right. She looked peaceful and . . .'

A little tear ran down her cheek before she said the last word.

'. . . dead.'

I didn't know what to say. What can you say?

'Dawn,' I said after a bit. 'In the dream she was her old self. She had the right lipstick. And her hair was the same as always. And she wore both shoes. And those leather gloves you gave her.'

Dawn suddenly gasped as if she had swallowed something that wouldn't go down. 'Mum only wore those gloves once,' she yelled. 'The day after her birthday. The day of the last bus trip. The one you can't remember. When Mum died. You must have been re-living the last journey.'

That made me stop and think. The germs in my mind must have made me believe that the bus was growing new again. And then I'd started to remember the last journey.

'What happened next?' Dawn yelled. 'Tell me.'

'I don't know,' I said. 'I jumped out of the bus and everything was back to normal.'

Dawn started to punch my pillow. I think she was pretending that it was me. 'Trust you,' said Dawn. 'Trust you to wake up just at the wrong moment. Can't you do anything right? You're just like your useless father.' She picked up my apple-man and threw him across the room.

'You ratbag,' I yelled. I grabbed her by the arm and gave her a bit of a shake. In a flash we were scratching and pulling and rolling over and over on the floor like two fiends.

She was too strong for me. She always got the better of me.

'Ugly step-sister,' I shouted.

'Ugly?' she yelled. 'Ugly? You should take a look at yourself.'

She suddenly let go of me and started backing away. Staring at me as if I had just landed from Mars.

'What's up now?' I spat out.

'Look in the mirror,' said Dawn in a horrified voice.

I stood up and stared into the mirror.

It wasn't me. The reflection belonged to someone else. A mean face. Sort of like a bully. A snarling, hateful vision of what I was feeling.

'Aagh,' I screamed. 'Aagh . . .'

'Calm down,' said Dawn. 'Calm down. It's the infection. Feeding on the anger. Think of peaceful things.'

I closed my eyes and tried to think of something relaxing. It's hard to be calm when you have just turned into a monster. 'Think,' I said to myself. 'Think peace.' I tried to force pleasant images into my mind. The moon reflected in a silver pond . . . a hamburger . . . gentle sea breezes . . . a trail bike roaring through the forest . . . a waterfall . . . a bucket of ice-cream. Gradually my breathing slowed and my heart stopped its hammering.

'That's better,' said Dawn. 'Keep it up. It's working.'

I opened my eyes and examined my reflection. The hateful face was draining away. I was coming back to normal. I felt a little better. I couldn't get rid of the fear though. And it still showed in my face. But fear isn't as ugly as hate and I didn't look nearly as bad as before.

'Dawn,' I said. 'Whenever I get angry the illness starts

to spread in my body and changes my looks. It's the same with Mum. Did you see her ugly face when she told you off?'

'You'll have to keep your cool,' said Dawn. 'Otherwise you'll stir it up again.'

'Then don't rubbish my dad,' I said. 'He wouldn't send germs. He doesn't know anything about it.'

Dawn was staring down at the floor with a startled look on her face. 'He might not know anything about the slobberers,' she said. 'But the slobberers sure know about him.'

She pointed to a silvery trail on the floor. It looked like a snail's track. But we both knew that it wasn't. It was the trail left the day before by the last slobberer out of the apple. The long, long one. The one that had spelt out a word with its body.

We both stood there in silence. My secret was out. The silvery trail spelt out the word Karl for anyone to see.

'He didn't send the slobberers,' I shrieked.

'All right, all right,' said Dawn. 'Maybe he did and maybe he didn't. But there's one thing for sure. If he didn't, the next creature that gets infected is going to go looking for him.'

She was right. She was dead right. If Mum infected any living creature, it was going to make Dad its victim.

The slobberer's message said so.

I jumped to my feet and ran to the window. Outside in the forest were all sorts of animals. And insects. Mum could infect any of them.

I felt like a paper-clip between two big magnets. I wanted to stay and protect Mum. Keep creatures away from her. But I wanted to go to Dad too. Mum might already have infected something that was on its way to Dad.

Mum. Dad. Mum. Dad. How could I choose? In the end I decided to try and help Dad. After all, Mum had Jack to look after her. Dad might not have anybody. And I hadn't seen him for so long.

'We have to find him,' I said. 'We have to find Dad before it's too late.'

'Does Eileen know where he is?' said Dawn.

'No. He never told us. We'll have to find him our-selves. Let's go.'

A hand grabbed my arm. A powerful hand. It was Jack. 'The only place you're going, young man,' he said, 'is to hospital.'

The staff at our local hospital were having a quiet afternoon. Until we walked in.

'Yuck,' said the young doctor in Casualty when he saw Rory and Eileen's skin, which I thought was a bit slack for a person with years of training.

The doctor asked Rory and Eileen if they'd been in contact with acid or crop-dusting spray or sewage. Eileen looked bewildered. 'I don't think so,' she said.

Rory didn't say anything. I could see he was trying hard not to get angry, but he looked pretty trapped and unhappy.

He put his mouth close to my ear, which felt a bit strange. 'Help me get out of here,' he hissed.

'Please.'

Dad explained about the car crash and the step-family and the stress. 'Stress-induced skin complaint, I reckon,' he said to the doctor. 'Plus Eileen's probably got a bit of concussion.'

'From the war,' said Gramps. 'Against the green army.'

The doctor asked Dad if Gramps had concussion too. 'No,' said Dad, 'he's just old.'

I squeezed Gramps' hand.

The doctor took Rory and Eileen off for tests, and Dad for a leg x-ray. As they were going, Rory grabbed my arm. 'Please,' he whispered desperately.

I didn't say anything.

As I watched them go I struggled with my second shameful thought that day. What if the doctors couldn't find out what the infection was? What if Rory and Eileen were shut away and kept under observation for weeks or months or years?

That would just leave me and Dad and Gramps. And Dad would go back to hugging me first.

I tried hard not to feel too happy. It didn't seem right in a place where there were people with tubes up their noses. But I did feel my heart beat a bit faster and I did have a sudden urge to hug Gramps.

Then, as Rory was being led away down the corridor, he turned and looked at me. The look only lasted a few seconds, but it left me shaking. It was the look of a kid who wanted to save his dad. Not just a bit. Not even quite a lot.

Desperately.

And even though I didn't want to, I knew exactly how he felt.

I felt the same way every time I pictured myself sprawled on the floor watching a dopey TV show while Mum was drowning. Chuckling my head off. Instead of hurling myself out the door and sprinting to the river and diving in and saving her.

If only I could turn time back.

But I couldn't.

All I could save now was her good name. And my memories of her.

'Gramps,' I said. 'We've got to get Rory out of here.'

Gramps looked disappointed. He was fiddling with the postage stamp machine in the hospital foyer. 'I wanted some of that chocolate,' he said as I led him away. Then he frowned. 'Rory can't leave, he's sick. He needs to be cured.'

'He will be, Gramps,' I said. 'But first we've got to find out what type of infection he's got and I reckon the person to tell us that is Rory's dad.'

Gramps peered into the distance as if he was struggling with a memory. Perhaps it was just the chocolate.

'I dunno,' he said after a bit. 'Doctors are the ones that know about infections. And vets.'

'Gramps,' I said, looking hard into his milky grey eyes. 'I think Rory can help us find out about Mum.'

Gramps' wobbly jaw was suddenly set hard. 'My daughter is dead,' he croaked, 'and I won't hear a bad word against her.'

'Me neither,' I said. 'That's why we've got to get Rory out of here. You know how the infection is taking Eileen's memory away? Well I think it's bringing Rory's back. He's started having memories of being on the bus just before it crashed. If we can give him the chance, he might be able to tell us why Mum died.'

Gramps' eyes shone. Then his shoulders slumped. 'It's hopeless,' he said. 'This place is like a fortress. The staff have all got guns.'

I reminded him about the difference between guns and pagers, then told him my plan. His eyes shone again.

'There's an op-shop next door,' he said. 'We can get the stuff we need there.'

After we'd been to the op-shop, we waited in the hospital foyer until the nurse on reception ducked out to get some afternoon tea. Then we hurried along the corridor. I looked at the signs on the walls and doors.

'What's the word,' I whispered, 'for the place people are put when they've got an infectious disease?'

'Dunno,' said Gramps. 'I'm no good at crosswords. How many letters?'

I saw a sign on a side corridor saying QUARANTINE.

It looked like the word.

Small country hospitals like ours didn't have many patients with infectious diseases, I could tell. The hand-written sign was one give-away. Another was the precautions they'd taken to keep the germs in. I'd seen on telly once how big city hospitals had double air-lock doors with a special microwave oven for your handbag. Our hospital just had big sheets of plastic sticky-taped across the corridor.

Holding our breath, Gramps and I squeezed through the plastic. No alarms went off. We gave each other relieved looks. Then suddenly a trolley burst through a door. Wheeling it was a bloke in a white smock. He stopped and looked at us suspiciously.

'What are you doing in here?' he demanded.

I turned Gramps around. 'Come on, Gramps,' I said crossly. 'You know you're not meant to be down here. The old people's ward is the other way.'

'Eh?' said Gramps.

I turned to the bloke. 'After you,' I said. 'He's a bit slow.'

The bloke gave me a sympathetic grin and clattered off through the plastic. We waited till he'd turned the corner, then hurried on down the corridor.

'Sorry,' I said to Gramps. 'You're not really slow.'

'That was a close one,' said Gramps. 'Ernie Piggot

went on one of those trolleys and lost his prostate.'

I took Mum's shoe out of my shirt and held it out to Gramps. 'Hang on to this,' I said. 'In case there are infectious germs in the air.'

Gramps took it. 'Thanks,' he said.

We started peeking through the glass panels in the doors. The first two rooms were empty. Then someone called my name. 'That sounded like Rory,' I whispered. The door of a nearby room clunked shut. 'In there,' I said.

We stepped into darkness. A tiny thread of sunlight peeped through the curtains. I could just make out the shape of a figure in the bed. I went over. Rory didn't move. I gave him a shake. Instead of flesh and bone, all I could feel were folds of something soft.

Skin.

I gasped and jumped back. Oh no. The infection had done what the slobberers hadn't been able to. Eaten out Rory's insides.

'Don't look,' I mumbled to Gramps, my head swimming with nausea and grief.

'That's right,' said a voice. 'Or the light'll hurt your eyes.' We spun round. A light blinked on and Rory stepped out of a little bathroom. 'They're just blankets,' he said, pointing to the bed. 'So they'll think I'm asleep after I've gone.' He sighed. 'Except I can't go 'cos they'll recognise me. Every doctor, nurse and handyman has been sticky-beaking through that door at the kid with the yucky skin.'

My heart had calmed down enough for me to speak. 'It's not that yucky,' I said, which wasn't true. I tried to ignore my neck cramp and all thoughts of curried-egg sandwiches. 'Anyway,' I went on, 'we've got a plan.' I handed him the op-shop bag. 'Put these on.'

Rory stared. 'That's a *woman's* coat,' he said indignantly. 'An *old* woman's coat.'

'That's right,' said Gramps. 'It was Ivy Bothwell's.'

'And this,' I said, 'is an old woman's hat. If you want to get out of here, put them on.'

Scowling, Rory put them on. 'This is pointless,' he said. 'They'll still recognise my face.'

'No they won't,' I said.

Rory rolled his eyes. 'You're so dumb,' he said.

I took a deep breath. This was the riskiest part of the plan. 'Not as dumb as you,' I said. 'You think the sun shines out of your dad's bum, but a two year old could see he's the evil mastermind behind everything that's happened.'

Rory's eyes flashed angrily. 'No he's not,' he snapped. His face was starting to change.

'It's obvious,' I said. 'Your dad's using this infection to get back at you and Eileen for being in a new family.'

'Bull,' hissed Rory. Already he was hardly recognisable.

'He's out to get you,' I said as harshly as I could.

'Shut up,' gritted Rory, furious. His face had crumpled into a creased, wizened mask of anger. In the hat and coat he looked like grumpy old Mrs Creely from the school tuck shop.

I felt terrible that I'd done it to him. But this was no time for guilt.

'Quick,' I said to Gramps. 'Let's get him out of here.'

I grabbed Rory's overnight bag and turned the light off and we crept out and hurried down the corridor and through the plastic. Gramps was great, keeping an eye out for doctors so I could concentrate on saying awful things to Rory about his dad to keep him angry.

Only once did Gramps lose it. Just as we were hurrying out to the car park, he looked at Rory, confused. 'Mrs Creely,' he said, 'what are you in for?'

By the time we got to Gramps' car, Rory was back to normal. Well, as normal as a kid with a monstrous infection could be.

He looked at me. 'Thanks,' he said. 'I know you had to do that, and I know you didn't really mean it.'

I didn't say anything.

'Thanks, Gramps,' said Rory. 'I don't know what I'd

do without you.' He and Gramps hugged each other for a long time. I looked away. Sometimes, I thought, too much hugging goes on in this family.

Rory suddenly had a thought. 'I should say goodbye to Mum,' he said.

'No,' I said. 'That wouldn't be a good idea.' I'd had the same thought about Dad but it was too risky. 'They're in good hands,' I said.

Then I had another thought. I almost kicked myself.

'Worm Boy,' I said. 'You don't know where your dad is, do you?'

Rory stopped hugging Gramps. 'No,' he said. 'You know I don't.'

'So how are we going to find him?' I asked.

Rory gave one of those grins small kids give when they've had a really good idea. 'We'll get ourselves a guide,' he said, and then grinned even wider because I didn't have a clue what he was talking about. 'If my mum infects something,' he continued, 'that thing will go straight to Dad, right? To try and infect him.'

'Probably,' I said.

'So we get my mum to infect something,' he said, 'then follow it.'

I stared at him. The germ was obviously getting to his brain. Even Gramps could see how dopey that idea was.

'What do we follow it in?' I said. 'A helicopter? You saw how fast those slobberers moved.'

'Yeah,' said Rory. 'That's why we need something slow.'

He opened Gramps' car door, groped around on the floor and held up the plastic box with the see-through lid.

'Something slow like this,' he said. Inside the box, the snail looked at us, bored.

'Clever boy,' said Gramps. I scowled. The trouble with old people was they were too easily impressed.

'Two things, Wonder Boy,' I said. 'One, this snail will take about eighteen years to get anywhere. Two, it'll infect every other snail it meets on the way.'

'Not if we keep it in the box,' said Rory. 'The infected snail will be quarantined in here, and we can use it like a compass. Whichever direction the snail crawls, we drive.'

'Brilliant,' said Gramps. It was sickening. But I had to admit it was clever.

Except for one thing.

'How do we get your mum to infect it?' I said. 'We can't just go up to her and say, 'Excuse me, Eileen, can we put this snail on one of your scabs?'

'You and Gramps will have to do it,' said Rory. 'I can't go back in there.' He sighed. 'Do it gently.'

I sighed too, for my sake rather than Eileen's. Then I took Mum's shoe back from Gramps and told him to stay in the car with Rory. No point in us both being arrested for illegally touching a public hospital patient with a gastropod.

Eileen's room was down the corridor from Rory's. When I got there and peeked in, it was empty. I crept in, made sure nobody was in the bathroom, took the snail out of the box and started searching the room for blood samples or scabs.

Nothing.

Then I heard voices coming down the corridor.

I looked frantically around for a hiding place big enough for a girl and a snail. The bathroom was too risky. Coffee drinkers always had over-active bladders. I climbed into the wardrobe and hoped Eileen wasn't planning to change for dinner.

I'd just got the wardrobe doors closed when Eileen and a nurse came in. Through the crack I saw the nurse settle Eileen into bed and give her a tablet. 'This'll help you sleep,' she said. I hoped she was right. My heart was pounding and the snail was feeling very slimy in my hand.

After about ten years, Eileen's slow breathing told me she was asleep. I crept out of the wardrobe and checked her over. All her cuts and scratches were bandaged. I swallowed nervously. I'd have to make one of my own.

I searched among the nurse's stuff on the bedside table for a scalpel. Nothing. Not even a pair of scissors. Then I remembered something.

Mum's shoe had a loose nail in the heel. After a bit of a struggle I got it out with my teeth. It was pretty rusty but the tip was still fairly sharp. I rubbed it on my shirt so Eileen wouldn't get tetanus and wondered if I could get it through her skin without waking her up.

Eileen murmured something and rolled over. I could see her bare bottom through the crack in her hospital gown.

'Sorry, Eileen,' I whispered, and placed the point of the nail against her buttock.

I couldn't do it.

It was dopey. All the times I'd imagined stabbing my step-mother, and now I had the chance I couldn't even prick her skin.

Then I remembered something else. Eileen's feet. She was always complaining how her shoes rubbed her feet.

Carefully I lifted the sheet at the bottom of the bed. Perfect. Raw patches on both Eileen's heels.

'Sorry, snail,' I whispered and put it onto one of the

raw spots. I'd never infected a snail before so I didn't know how long it would take. I counted to ten, lifted the snail off, put it in the box, found band-aids on the bedside table, stuck one on each of Eileen's heels and slipped out of the room.

I hurried back to the car park with the world's first living compass inside my shirt. I tried to forget that the snail clinging to the thin plastic next to my skin was infected. I tried to forget what that could mean.

The whole way, though, I gripped Mum's shoe tightly.

Just in case.

quickly changed out of Ivy Bothwell's clothes. Then I hid inside the car with Gramps. There was no sign of Dawn. 'I hope she hasn't been taken,' whispered Gramps.

'She wouldn't tell the doctors what we're up to, would she?' I asked.

Gramps scoffed loudly. 'A Finnigan would never go over to the other side,' he said.

We had to get out of the hospital car park quickly before someone saw me and took me back into the isolation ward. In the distance I could see men in white coats searching. There was no time to lose. 'I'll do one quick whip round the grounds,' I said. 'And then we'll have to go without her.'

Gramps nodded. 'Watch out for sentries,' he said. 'And take these for the barbed wire.' He reached down under the seat and handed me a pair of pliers. Poor old Gramps. He thought he was back in the war again.

I slipped out of the car and started to run. Crash. I bumped into someone running just as fast in the other direction and we both sprawled onto the ground.

'Idiot,' said a familiar voice.

It was Dawn. She rubbed her big backside and grinned at me.

'Did you infect the snail?' I said hoarsely.

'The snail,' yelled Dawn. We both looked around. The lid had come off the box and the snail was heading across the car park at great speed. I had never seen a snail move so fast before. It was really travelling. I jumped up and ran after it with the box. I grabbed the snail by the shell and dropped it back inside the container and shoved the lid on.

'It must be infected,' said Dawn in amazement. 'A normal snail can't move that fast. You shouldn't have touched it.'

'It's okay,' I said. 'It's after Dad, not me. Let's go.'

I grabbed the front doorhandle of the Morris Minor with trembling fingers.

So did Dawn.

'I'm sitting in the front,' we both yelled at the same time.

I couldn't believe it. In the middle of all this excitement she was worrying about something as trivial as that.

And I knew why. She was jealous of me and Gramps. We were becoming mates. And Dawn didn't like it.

Dawn shoved me aside and jumped into the front seat of the car with Gramps. Oh well, I still had my apple-man for company. And the snail for that matter.

I shrugged and scrambled into the back. Gramps crunched the gears and the car lurched forward. Blue smoke billowed out behind us.

'Which way is the snail headed?' Gramps yelled.

I stared down into the snail box. The snail was moving fast. 'That way,' I said.

Gramps threw a glance over his shoulder. 'North-west,' he said.

The snail reached the end of the box and stopped. I turned the whole thing around and the snail immediately turned and headed north-west again.

Gramps accelerated noisily down the hospital drive and stopped at the road. 'Now which way?' he said.

The snail was still headed north-west which was lucky because the street ran in the same direction. 'Turn left,' I yelled.

Gramps followed my outstretched hand and the car lurched and swayed down the road. He was a terrible driver. He narrowly missed an old lady who was crossing the road. Then he stopped at a T-intersection.

This time we were not so lucky. The road ran from east to west.

'I don't know which way,' I yelled.

Gramps stared down at the snail. 'A strange compass,' he said. 'Must be captured from the enemy. It's not one of ours. But don't worry. They all work the same way. We just make every turn that takes us in the general direction. In the end we'll get there.'

Gramps lurched off to the right.

I looked at the snail. 'It's so creepy,' I said.

We both stared into the snail box. The snail looked normal but we knew it was intelligent now it was infected. It moved too fast. And those eyes. They were big. More like people's eyes. They swivelled on the end of their thin stalks. They looked back up at us. Filled with hate.

Dawn thought about it for a bit. 'All the infected creatures got smart,' she said. 'The sheep and the slobberers and the frogs. They all did clever things.'

'It's not the creatures,' I said. 'It's the germs. The germs take over their brains. This is not really a snail any more. It is only the body of a snail.'

I started to get scared. Very scared. 'Hey, Dawn?'

'What?'

'The frogs grew big.'

'Yeah?'

'So did the slobberers. And the sheep grew steel wool.'

'So?'

'So what's this snail going to do? Why is it just walking around inside the box? Why isn't it changing? Why doesn't it try to get out?'

'Because we are taking it to where it wants to go,' said Dawn. 'To your father. To the one next to you in the blood line. So it can infect him.'

She was right. Or was she? There was something that didn't make sense but I couldn't figure out what it was.

I had something else to worry about. The disease had infected me. And my mother. So what happened to the infected people? The virus fed on anger. We knew that. But in the end what became of the victims?

I tried not to think about it. But I couldn't help it.

'I'm going to die,' I blurted out.

Dawn reached over and put her hand on my arm. Even though I was panicking a little thrill ran through my body. She had a really soft hand for such a tough girl.

Gramps snatched a quick glance at me. 'Everybody dies sooner or later,' he said. 'It's just a matter of when.'

'That's okay if you're a hundred and fifty,' I said. 'But

I'm only thirteen. There's still a few things I haven't done yet.'

'Like what?' said Gramps.

I stared at Dawn. She really did have a cute little turned-up nose. And very nice lips. I could feel my face starting to go red. 'Like nothing,' I said grumpily.

Gramps gave a smile. 'There's plenty of things I still want to do, too,' he said.

'Like what?' said Dawn.

'Like never you mind,' he said with a devilish grin.

'He's thinking about Mrs Mugavin at the bowls club,' said Dawn.

'I am not,' said Gramps hotly. Then he started to chuckle. 'Okay, you got me,' he said.

Gramps was great. He cheered us up without us noticing that he had done it. A little bit of the terror had gone out of the journey.

The snail crawled about in the box. And the Morris Minor crawled along the roads.

We followed that snail. Out into the country. Far, far, from home. The sun was just beginning to set as we reached the town of Mooraboolie.

Gramps stopped at a roundabout. 'This is a big town,' he said. 'What does the snail say?'

'Left,' I said. 'It's the only road running north-west.'

The more I thought about it, the more scared I

became. At any moment I might see my dad. That was wonderful. I'd waited so long. But . . .

'What will the snail do when we get there?' I asked in a trembling voice. 'What if it bursts out of its box?'

Gramps changed the subject. 'We had snails in France,' he said. 'During the war. Do you know what we used to do with them? When we were short of rations . . .'

Gramps never got to tell us the rest. We passed under a sign which said AMBLE-BY COTTAGES. Gramps threw a glance at the sign and put his foot on the brake. I looked ahead and saw that the road came to a dead end. We were in a sort of crescent that ended in a circle.

I stared out of the window. There were lots of kids riding bikes and skateboards and mucking around on the footpath. More kids than you would normally see in a street like that. There was something different about them. What was it? Then I realised. They were all dressed alike. Not the same clothes. But the same *sort* of clothes. As if they had been bought in the one shop.

Gramps was looking at them too. With a horrified expression on his face. Suddenly he let out the clutch and did a u-turn. The Morris Minor bumped up over the kerb and started heading back the way we had come. Gramps had a wild, upset look in his eye.

'Hey,' I yelled. 'This isn't the way. The snail wants to go back there.'

The snail was going crazy. It was foaming with green bubbles and racing in circles inside the cake box. Its eyes blinked and winked angrily. It wanted to get out.

'I've just remembered something your mum . . .' said Gramps. 'I made a mistake. You don't use the enemy's compass.'

I reached over and turned off the ignition key. 'We're close to Dad,' I shouted. 'You're not stopping me now.' I jumped out of the car and checked the snail. It wanted me to go along the street. I ran, faster and faster. My heart was thumping. At any moment I would see Dad. My father. Who loved me.

Suddenly the snail stopped. Not a movement.

I was standing next to a large tree on the nature strip outside a house. I gave the box a shake. 'Which way,' I yelled. 'Which way?'

The snail started to climb up the side of the box. This was crazy. Was it trying to get out? Did it want to streak ahead and infect my father?

'Turn it on its side,' said a sad voice. It was Gramps. Dawn wasn't far behind him.

I turned the box on its side and the snail immediately started climbing.

'Up?' I said. 'It wants to go up?'

I looked into the tree. The leaves and branches were thick and I couldn't see into the top. I started to climb. It was difficult going. I had the slobberer's wound on one hand, a snail box in the other and the apple-man half hanging out of my pocket. But I climbed and climbed and climbed.

I was desperate. Branches scratched my face and sharp twigs clawed at my legs. But I ignored them. I didn't even notice my bleeding legs and fingers. All I wanted was to see my father again. Dad, Dad, Dad.

Finally, right at the top, I stopped. There was someone there. Sitting on a branch.

A head popped out between the leaves and looked my way.

My heart dropped. It wasn't Dad.

It was a boy. He was older than me. He stared at me with wide open eyes. For a moment he was frozen. Stunned. He looked at me wordlessly. He seemed to be choking with shock. He couldn't believe what he was seeing.

Neither could I.

The snail box slipped from my hand and tumbled down through the branches. I hardly noticed. I didn't even hear it hit the ground. And I didn't look down to see if the lid had come off the box.

RORY

I couldn't take my gaze off the boy. I had seen those big, brown eyes before. And that gap between the two front teeth. And the nose and the hair. And the ears. I had seen them all. In the mirror.

The boy in the branches. Staring into my eyes.

Was a dead ringer for me.

To be continued in ...

④ Dead Ringer

Read this excerpt from the next exciting instalment in the *Wicked!* serial

It was like looking into a mirror. The boy who stared at me through the tree branches had my eyes, and ears, and hair. Even my nose. There was a bit of fuzz on his top lip. And he was a bit taller and had a couple of pimples.

But apart from that, the boy was me. He blinked back – stunned – not believing what he was seeing.

I tell you this. I had been chased by slobberers. And I had looked into the jaws of a giant frog. I had seen Dawn's dead mother smile at me.

And had followed a snail compass halfway across the state. But all that was nothing compared to this.

I knew this boy. And he knew me. But how can you know someone you have never seen before? And why was my stomach jumping? Why were my hands clammy?

I felt like you do on Christmas morning when you get an unexpected present. It was like witnessing a birth. Weird. Really weird.

'Aagh, the snail's out. The snail's escaped.' Dawn's shrieking voice came up from below.

I couldn't see the ground from where I was. But I realised with a shock that the infected snail must have escaped when I dropped the box. The snail that was seeking my next of kin. That wanted to kill my father.

'It's heading up the tree,' came Gramps' shaky shout. 'It's infiltrating our defences. Get the beggar.'

The boy was puzzled. But I was scared. Was my dad up there somewhere? I had to protect him. I scrambled out in the branches. 'Dad, Dad, Dad,' I yelled. 'Where are you? Look out. Jump. Get out of the tree. The snail's coming.'

ThE aUtHoRs

Paul Jennings and Morris Gleitzman
are Australia's most popular writers
for children. They are also very good
friends.

Now, for the first time, they are
writing together. Twice as weird,
twice as funny, twice as spooky, twice
as mind-blowing. If you loved their
books before, you'll love *Wicked!*
twice as much.

There's never been anything like it.

PaUL JeNniNGs

There are a lot of animals in my stories. That's because I have always had a lot of pets. Here are some of them:

I had a mouse called Nibbler, and a cat that wasn't called Singenpoo. I had dogs called Bing, Deefa (D for Dog), Sold, Skip and Sandy. And I had frogs. They ate each other. (Er . . . I mean they ate each other's food.)

People who have pets live longer than people who don't.

I must get another dog.

MorRiS GleiTZmaN

I have a lot of pets too – 634 of them (including three walruses). Here are a few other things you might not know about me:

Once I sticky-taped myself to the wing of a 747 and flew upside down to Caracas, I can speak sixteen languages all at once, my hobbies are cooking underwater and seeing how many bowling balls I can fit into my mouth, I've written 126,222,945 books and I live on Pluto.

Oh yes, and I like making up stories.

READ MORE IN PUFFIN

For children of all ages, Puffin represents quality and variety – the very best in publishing today around the world.

For complete information about books available from Puffin – and Penguin – and how to order them, contact us at the appropriate address below. Please note that for copyright reasons the selection of books varies from country to country.

On the worldwide web: www.puffin.co.uk

In the United Kingdom: Please write to *Dept. EP, Penguin Books Ltd, Bath Road, Harmondsworth, West Drayton, Middlesex UB7 ODA*

In the United States: Please write to *Consumer Sales, Penguin USA, P.O. Box 999, Dept. 17109, Bergenfield, New Jersey 07621-0120.* VISA and MasterCard holders call 1-800-253-6476 to order Penguin titles

In Canada: Please write to *Penguin Books Canada Ltd, 10 Alcorn Avenue, Suite 300, Toronto, Ontario M4V 3B2*

In Australia: Please write to *Penguin Books Australia Ltd, P.O. Box 257, Ringwood, Victoria 3134*

In New Zealand: Please write to *Penguin Books (NZ) Ltd, Private Bag 102902, North Shore Mail Centre, Auckland 10*

In India: Please write to *Penguin Books India Pvt Ltd, 706 Eros Apartments, 56 Nehru Place, New Delhi 110 019*

In the Netherlands: Please write to *Penguin Books Netherlands bv, Postbus 3507, NL-1001 AH Amsterdam*

In Germany: Please write to *Penguin Books Deutschland GmbH, Metzlerstrasse 26, 60594 Frankfurt am Main*

In Spain: Please write to *Penguin Books S. A., Bravo Murillo 19, 1° B, 28015 Madrid*

In Italy: Please write to *Penguin Italia s.r.l., Via Felice Casati 20, I–20124 Milano*

In France: Please write to *Penguin France S. A., 17 rue Lejeune, F–31000 Toulouse*

In Japan: Please write to *Penguin Books Japan, Ishikiribashi Building, 2–5–4, Suido, Bunkyo-ku, Tokyo 112*

In South Africa: Please write to *Longman Penguin Southern Africa (Pty) Ltd, Private Bag X08, Bertsham 2013*